DUTTON
CHILDREN'S BOOKS

An imprint of Penguin Group (USA) Inc.

LISA
CAMPBELL
ERNST

DUTTON CHILDREN'S BOOKS

A DIVISION OF PENGUIN YOUNG READERS GROUP

Published by the Penguin Group | Penguin Group (USA) Inc., 375 Hudson Street, New York, New York 10014, U.S.A. | Penguin Group (Canada), 90 Eglinton Avenue East, Suite 700, Toronto, Ontario M4P 2Y3, Canada (a division of Pearson Penguin Canada Inc.) | Penguin Books Ltd, 80 Strand, London WC2R 0RL, England | Penguin Ireland, 25 St Stephen's Green, Dublin 2, Ireland (a division of Penguin Books Ltd | Penguin Group (Australia), 250 Camberwell Road, Camberwell, Victoria 3124, Australia (a division of Pearson Australia Group Pty Ltd) | Penguin Books India Pvt Ltd, 11 Community Centre, Panchsheel Park, New Delhi - 110 017, India | Penguin Group (NZ), 67 Apollo Drive, Rosedale, North Shore 0632, New Zealand (a division of Pearson New Zealand Ltd) | Penguin Books (South Africa) (Pty) Ltd, 24 Sturdee Avenue, Rosebank, Johannesburg 2196, South Africa | Penguin Books Ltd, Registered Offices: 80 Strand, London WC2R 0RL, England

CIP Data is available.

Published in the United States by Dutton Children's Books,
a division of Penguin Young Readers Group
345 Hudson Street, New York, New York 10014
www.penguin.com/youngreaders

Designed by Heather Wood with Lisa Campbell Ernst

Manufactured in China | First Edition
ISBN 978-0-525-47873-7
10 9 8 7 6 5 4 3 2 1

Sylvia Jean

was a Pig Scout extraordinaire.
By day she memorized every rule and
regulation, secret sign and handshake.
By night she dreamed super-scout dreams,
still wearing her most prized possession,
the golden Pig Scout Snout pin.

A PIG SCOUT NEVER GIVES UP

Sylvia Jean's
favorite day was
Friday, when her Pig
Scout Troop met at
four o'clock sharp.
"Sylvia Jean,
reporting for duty!"
she announced.

"Attention, scouts!" called their leader, Miss Rose.
"Today we begin work on the most important badge of
all, the Good-Deed Badge. We will begin by having each
of you choose a good deed."

The troop gasped, Sylvia Jean
loudest of all.

"I'll plant flowers!" said Greta.
Too dirty, thought Sylvia Jean.

"I'll pick up trash!"
yelled June. *Too smelly,*
thought Sylvia Jean.

Stella would read
to toddlers. *Too wiggly.*

Grace would paint a neighbor's fence. *Too mess—*
HEY, *that neighbor idea is pretty good.*

Sylvia Jean jumped to
her feet, shouting. "I've got
it! My neighbor, old Mrs.
VanHooven! She twisted her
ankle and can't walk! I'll take
care of HER!

"Prepare to be amazed!" sang
Sylvia Jean.

Sylvia Jean gathered items for every possible need, from Band-Aids to balloons, tissues to tulips, pillows to puppets.

"I can't wait to see the look on Mrs. VanHooven's face!" Sylvia Jean crowed when she left her house the next morning. "She is so lucky!"

Instead of using the doorbell, Sylvia Jean blew her tuba, just in case Mrs. VanHooven was hard of hearing.

Silence.
Then a timid, "Who is it?"

"It's me, Sylvia Jean, the
answer to your prayers!"

Silence.
Then, "Come in?"

Sylvia Jean burst through the door. "HELLO!" she gushed. "I've come to nurse you back to health!"

Mrs. VanHooven's eyes grew big as Sylvia Jean told her about the Good-Deed Badge. "Th-thank you, dear," she stammered. "But please, all I need is rest."

"No, no, I insist!" Sylvia Jean said, speeding toward her patient. "Let me fluff those pillows—"

Suddenly, the tuba and supplies tipped.

Before Sylvia Jean could balance them,

her feet shot out from under her and she slipped—

straight toward Mrs. VanHooven.

They both screamed. Then, CRASH!
"Please, dear," whimpered Mrs. VanHooven. "Go."

Walking home, Sylvia Jean sniffed. "At least I took her mind off her ankle. Tomorrow's *got* to be better."

But by the time she reached her house, her mother had already received a call.

"I'm afraid the doctor has ordered you to stay away from Mrs. VanHooven. He says she's much too fragile for your kind of help."

"What?" Sylvia Jean cried. "That's impossible—she needs me!" She stomped to her room.

Sylvia Jean paced back and forth, mumbling to herself. "Sure, maybe I overdid it a smidge, but this is for a *badge*!" Remembering the badge, Sylvia Jean panicked. What would she do now?

"Calm down," Sylvia Jean told herself. She touched her Pig Scout Snout pin, and read it: A PIG SCOUT NEVER GIVES UP.

"Okay, then, think," she said. "I can't visit her, but anyone else can—even a total stranger."

Sylvia Jean began to laugh as she headed for her dress-up closet. "If total strangers can visit her, then strangers it will be," she announced.

The next morning a feeble-looking pig left Sylvia Jean's house with a golden snout pin in her pocket. She hobbled up the street to Mrs. VanHooven's door and knocked.

Silence.
Then, "Who is it?"
"I'm your new neighbor,
Mrs. Pink," said a creaky voice.
"Come in," called a weary
Mrs. VanHooven.

"Violets!" said Mrs. VanHooven. "My favorite! Are you sure we haven't met? You look familiar, somehow. . . ."

"Yes, yes, quite sure," Mrs. Pink said, turning around. "I must be going." And she ran out the door.

Mrs. VanHooven watched her new neighbor walk up the street. "That's odd," she said, seeing Mrs. Pink turn a perfect cartwheel.

The next day a very dashing-looking gentleman left Sylvia Jean's house, walked straight to Mrs. VanHooven's door, and knocked crisply.

"Who is it?" called Mrs. VanHooven.

"Your new neighbor from Spain, Señor Vía. I have brought you a dish of my famous Spanish rice and beans!"

"Do come in," said Mrs. VanHooven. "Oh, it smells heavenly!"

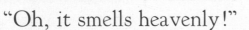

Señor Vía put the dish on the table.
"I will leave you now to rest," he said
with a deep bow. "Enjoy."

"What a lovely gentleman," Mrs. VanHooven said. She continued to watch him as he skipped all the way to Sylvia Jean's house.

"*Very* odd," she said, helping herself to the delicious food.

In the following days, Mrs. VanHooven watched as mysterious strangers left Sylvia Jean's house only to arrive at her front door, introducing themselves as new neighbors.

A cowboy—"Howdy, ma'am," —brought the newest book on the bestseller list: *High Noon at Pig Snout Corral.*

Miss Monique, a ballerina from France, brought chocolate truffles. "Zee sweets for zee sweet!" she sang.

And an artist, Mr. Cool, brought a painting.

"My, this neighborhood gets more interesting every day!" Mrs. VanHooven said as the last visitor, a Viking princess, quickly left.

With each passing day, Mrs. VanHooven's ankle grew a little stronger, and she grew a little more puzzled—until the day she saw something shiny on the floor. Examining it, the old pig chuckled.

By Thursday, Sylvia Jean was about to burst. "I did it!" she sang, "I did my good deed, and Mrs. VanHooven never knew it was me!" She sashayed around the room. "I deserve *two* badges for this!"

Sylvia Jean pulled out the badge form. "Now to fill this in!" she announced, her fanciest pen poised to write.

EXPLAIN YOUR PROJECT, the form read.

And then it hit her. "*I can't.*" she said. "I *can't* tell anyone. The doctor told me to stay away, and I disobeyed. If I confess that, they'll never give me the badge—they might even kick me out of the troop!"

A small cry escaped her lips. Sylvia Jean could share nothing at the meeting tomorrow and would watch, disgraced, as the other scouts received their badges.

She fell into a deep despair that followed her like a black cloud to the next day's Pig Scout meeting.

That afternoon, the scouts were atwitter. Everyone was anxious to share their glorious deeds. Each took a turn until only Sylvia Jean remained.

"Sylvia Jean?" Miss Rose said. "You may go next."

She stood, staring at the floor silently. Her eyes burned with tears. "I, I can't, I didn't . . ."

"Want to brag," came a voice.

Everyone turned to see Mrs. VanHooven hobbling forward on crutches.

"Sylvia Jean is far too kind to brag," Mrs. VanHooven continued, "but she arranged to have the most *fascinating* characters visit me while I was laid up. She is an angel. An absolute angel."

The troop clapped as the older pig hugged her young neighbor.

Sylvia Jean turned three shades of pink, and then whispered, "How did you know?"

Mrs. VanHooven handed her something shiny—Sylvia Jean's golden Pig Scout Snout pin.

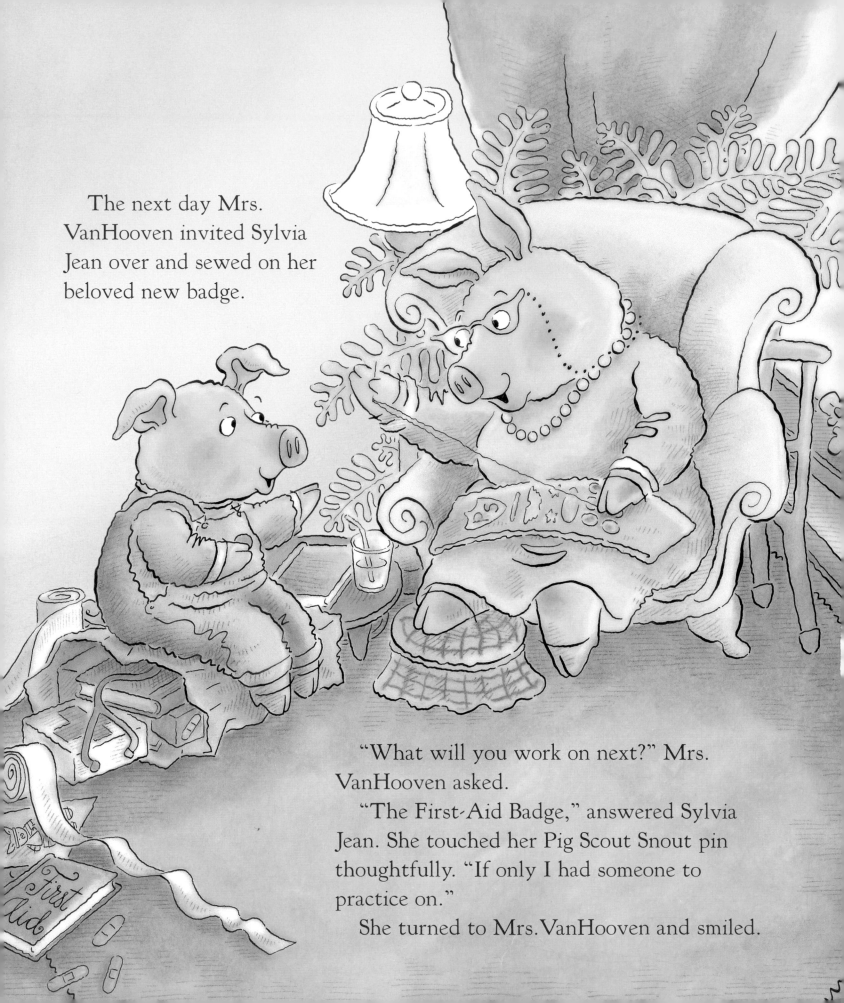

The next day Mrs. VanHooven invited Sylvia Jean over and sewed on her beloved new badge.

"What will you work on next?" Mrs. VanHooven asked.

"The First-Aid Badge," answered Sylvia Jean. She touched her Pig Scout Snout pin thoughtfully. "If only I had someone to practice on."

She turned to Mrs. VanHooven and smiled.